Mississippi And New York City

An Urban Novel

By

D1490764

Author Larry Earl Toombs

I would like to dedicate New York

And Mississippi to my childhood

friend who I loved and I lost Rest

Well Donnell Trotter.

Cp1. Mississippi Meets New York City

It was on a hot summer's day when the two guys named Mississippi and New York City met ironically on a street named Mississippi. The two never met each other a day in their lives. The two started a conversation after Mississippi said aloud, "This is my street because my name is Mississippi."

New York overheard him and said, "Well this is my city because my name is New York." Mississippi spoke with a heaven southern accent, he was from Greenville Mississippi even though he spoke with a heavy accent he was very intelligent and smart.

New York was a white slim guy about 33 years of age and his new friend Mississippi was near the same age, he was an African American Guy. The two became acquainted with each another very fast. Their persona's and attitudes was nearly the same. The duo became very bonded with each other. They both were unemployed at the time but their work history was fine, they both had been locked up in jail before for petty crimes but neither one had a felon.

The street life affected Mississippi in the south so he moved to Manhattan New York to seek a better life and likewise his friend. The two were looking for fast money because they needed it so they applied for work at a temp agency. Mississippi was also known as "Sip," So one-day Sip and New York gathered their information together such as social security card and id and they both entered the temp agency office to apply for work. Sip didn't have his driver's license to apply for work so the attendant at the temp office denied his application for work until he noticed that New York and Mississippi were black and white friends who came there together.

New York didn't have his license either to qualify for employment either so the white supervisor didn't deny New York and since he saw them together he gave Sip the job too. Eventually the pair knew what they had to do to make it in New York City. Mississippi known as Sip knew he had to help New York in the black Community and New York had to help Sip survive in the white neighborhood, it all sounded like a good plan and worked out very fine.

The job was going very well for the both of them. Finally, they were getting the amount of money they needed to survive because each of them had child support to pay. In the state of New York, the law stated that if a person does not work to pay the child support they would face criminal charges or have to pay a fine. Neither of the guys wanted to do time in jail after all they were responsible parents who loved their children and wanted to accept the responsibility to take care of their children.

Mississippi has a girl about one-year-old and New York has two children, one girl and a boy nearly a year apart. The job supervisor became attached to both the guys especially Sip because he was from the south and he loved to work hard, the boss eventually made him the lead supervisor on his production line. New York was a hard worker too but he only wanted to work the minimum amount of hour he needed to survive.

Soon the pair was able to afford to buy their own two-bedroom apartment, which allowed their kids to be comfortable.

Child support was being collected from the both of them on time however Sip was not with his baby mother and she was in a relationship with another man. Even though he paid the child support, his ex-girlfriend would not often bring his baby girl to visit him.

He went down to the social security office and

made a complaint that he was paying 400 dollars a month and still was not able to see his child.

It was protocol that the social security office contacts the mother of his daughter and ask her why she wouldn't allow Sip to see his daughter after all he was paying child support. It became relevant what the real problem was, his little daughter mother was named Aliyah she picked up the phone to answer the call from the social security office and her very jealous boyfriend overheard the conversation with the office.

He snatched the phone out of her hand and said, "He was Amanda's father now and she was not going to see any other so called father," He snatched the phone away from her. Amanda's stepfather name was Jimmy who immediately responded boisterous and asked Aliyah, "Was she still in love with Mississippi of course she responded, "No." Well Jimmy was a real nut job especially after he had finished a twelve-year stint in a New York Penitentiary.

Jimmy grabbed his handgun from the dresser drawer and explained to his now girlfriend Aliyah, "If she talks to Sip or goes anywhere around him or even let Amanda see him he would kill her and the baby. He had threatened her before this is the reason the baby mother would not let her baby see the real biological father Sip.

The next day at the temp agency, the two guys reported for duty. Sippi was telling New York about his problem, explaining to him that he pays child support to the child support office and he can't see Amanda.

New York told Sip that in most cases it is not the mother of the child who stops the child from seeing the father, it could be a jealous stepfather.

Mississippi explained to New York that he was going by the couple's house to see Amanda. He hadn't saw his two-year-old baby girl and it was just tearing him apart not to see her.

The desperate father said he needed to see his little girl before she forgets all about him. Sip further said, "This is what they want me to do forget about my baby and hope she forgets about me."

His very good friend told Sippi, "I don't think it is a good idea to go by there and see her." "If I was you I would wait until this all clears up and let her come to you." His friend replied, "If I wait too long I want have a daughter, I just can't wait."

Once again, New York explained to Sip what could happen if he shows up over there. If you go over there the law won't be on your side and somebody could get hurt if you just show up unannounced.

The two guys left the temp agency, it was time to go home. While at home trying to pray to God to make a way for him to see his little daughter Amanda, it wasn't enough. Precious moments the parent shared with his little daughter was ravishing through his head and this overtook Sip.

He grabbed a handgun out of the drawer and went unannounced to his baby girl's house. Once he made his arrival, he knocked on the door and Jimmy answered the door and asked the knocker, "Who was he looking for?"

The stepfather had never saw Sip's face before However before jimmy could answer he saw Amanda his step daughter in her biological's dad face and said, "you must be a fool to come here, I will put you in your place and you will never go anyplace again Amanda is my daughter you creep." He didn't realize how much Mississippi had lost it, during the argument sip went into his pocket to retrieve a forty-five automatic handgun.

The two struggled over the pistol until finally Sip shot Jimmy one time after the first shot, he realized he was wrong and his mind snapped back to reality but it was too late. He was already guilty of attempted murder and trespassing so he ran and jumped into his car and made a getaway but not before the neighbor wrote his make of the car and jotted his license place down which later was given to the New York Metropolitan Police.

Aliyah Amanda's mother was under the very loud hair dryer placed over her head, she did not hear the shot but her little daughter heard it.

Amanda could speak very well at two years old, she explained to her that Jimmy was lying on the front porch bleeding. In a haste, her mother frantically ran to the front door to find her boyfriend lying in a pool of blood. She checked his pulse the neighbor who wrote sip's License plates down informed her she had already dialed 911 and the police were on the way.

Very shortly, the medical team unit arrived

followed by a squat of police officer who had their weapons already drawn for this violent scene.

The police officers took down information that was vital in the case, they also interviewed the woman witness next door who volunteered and gave her information about Sip, hoping it would be a great clue to lead to his arrest. Yellow ribbon tape was placed around the couple's home after the incident that read, "Police Line Do Not Cross."

The next day at the job New York showed up with his lunch box as usually as the hour passed he noticed he did not see his loyal friend. He shrugged it off by saying in his head, "My partner just took an off day, and everyone is entitled to an off day."

Everything was going fine until the boss called

New York in the office to give him his next assignment when he overheard an incoming call coming from New York Metropolitan precinct. It was Sip, explaining he had been arrested and he couldn't show up for work and he didn't know how long he would be detained in Jail. He also explained that the guy he shot is on life support and if he dies he could end up spending the rest of his life in jail.

New York couldn't wait to get off work but what could he do? He could not bail out his pal because he had to give the money to his wife for his child, his method of payment for child support was with a money order which was agreed by the state of New York. Surprising the charges that Mississippi had obtained his bail was very low. Mainly the reason for the low bail arrangement was because, Sip did the crime in a predominately black neighborhood whose police district was already struggling with money being stolen from the last alderman and to be honest the city didn't even care and was looking for a reason to release him due to not being able to afford to house him. It was black on black crime which the city was very affiliated with and was tired and unconcerned with black on black crime. The New York City police department set his bail for only $800 dollars.

The second reason for the low bail release is Mississippi threw away the gun he shot Jimmy with. The couple house who he entered didn't testify against him and the surveillance camera was not even working. The only lead they had on Mississippi for the shooting was the neighbor next door who immediately detracted her story as soon as she found out, she was testifying all on her own. She told the police, "Well if the baby mother want say nothing, I won't say nothing either maybe one day she will learn some sense."

Once New York was situated, he called the N. Y. precinct and spoke to an officer. It was ironic he was talking to his long time relative who had recently taken the job and was captain of the precinct so he offered to pull some strings for New York. Remember earlier I explained to you that New York was white, upon arriving at the N.Y. precinct He saw his partner who was Captain Walker, he was also a white guy.

He called New York into a private room and

reduced again Sip's bond to only three-hundred dollars this allowed him to be bonded out immediately. Once the paperwork was finished the two guys Sip and New York was united. Mississippi apologized to his friend for not listening to him and going over the couple's house where his baby girl lived.

New York didn't change a word all he told Sip was, "See you at work tomorrow and you owe me one." Sippi replied, "No problem you got it." Jimmy began to progress from the gunshot wound and was able to talk, he was taking off life support. When his sister visited him, she told him Aaliyah had moved out of the house and had taken Amanda with her and she never wanted to see him again.

Jimmy healed up and was discharged from the hospital. He saw a letter by the bed that read, "Sorry he got shot but she couldn't go on with her life with a bully also a controlling man and do not try to find her because she didn't love him anymore." He eventually healed up but nothing could ever heal his permanent broken heart. Even though Sip was released on very low bond, he still had to stand trial for the alleged shooting, the details involved was not reliable so the courts probably would let him go free. The word was out on the street that even though he was released on a low bail, it would not be good for him to request a court appointed lawyer but he didn't have any choice since he didn't have any money.

The courts were sure to lose him a black man

standing trial with very little money and could spend at least twenty-five years to life without a witness but the stakes changed because now Jimmy, the guy he shot was fully recovered and he could now identify the shooter himself.

New York told Sip, "Buddy I have a strategic plan to save you from prison are you down?" Sip said, "Yea if it could save my black behind." New York replied, "I have cousin who is not an attorney at all. She practiced a little law before she got on drugs, I can get her to represent you." Sippi replied, "If she is on drugs how is she going to help me?"

She is not registered with any bar association so how is she going to help me. New York replied, "Do you want to do twenty-five to life." Sip replied, "No I don't, go get her to represent me." New York explained to his white cousin Amy who was pretending to be Sip's lawyer what she had to do or say to get his African American partner off the hook for the shooting case.

He explained to her please do not do any drugs the morning of the trial on June 16, 2022 because you must maintain a nice professional appearance. New York's friend Amy was a drug attic but she knew what she had to do to free Sip. The morning of the trial Amy was a sober as she could get but could she hold out before needing more drugs.

It was a perfect plan also New York was in the court room to help his friend. She looked very professional, she had a very beautiful dress also she wore makeup and carried a brief case. Amy looked so professional, that no one in the court room asked her which lawyer agency she was affiliated with. The so-called attorney was already briefed on what to say in order to get Mississippi of the hook.

Everything went fine Amy in her closing arguments asked for the full acquittal of her client, she maintained he is an innocent black man being discriminated by the judicial system. She also explained this is the reason society has written off African Americans today.

No one was suspected she was not a real lawyer, she was successful and her client was released with a clear record and was not placed on any papers or backed up any time.

The judge heard the touching testimony from her in favor of her client therefore the judge ordered the full release of Sip and he was allowed to return to work. Jimmy the African American who got shot did try to maintain a good defense but it was no good, his word fell upon deaf ears and Sippi was a free man.

The both of them thanked Amy and encouraged her to go to rehab and get help. Mississippi offered to pay for her rehabilitation and she refused. She was paid in cash and later overdosed off fentanyl in an abandoned building in downtown New York.

Sip was glad to be a free man even though Amy was not a real lawyer he found out she was a real person so he paid for all her funeral expenses. Life went on as usual working at the temp service day in and day out until now it was about to be a complete reversal in the story. Well everything went on as planned, ironically now Sip can see his daughter on a regular basic. There were certain places a white person wasn't accepted in New York but having an African American partner like Sip he could go anywhere he wanted to, the pair needed each other. Life was about to bring some challenging consequences for these two guy in the future so they have to learn to cling to each other.

Ch. 2. New York Discovers He Has A Son!

New York was having a great time living the perfect life at the temporary worker Agency. He had been promoted to full time along with his friend Mississippi who was working in a different department at this time but it had been a three-year anniversary for the two friends who seemed to be living a normal life up until this point. I mean both of the guys had perfect attendance on the job so they were promoted to supervisor in different departments.

It was quitting time at the job and the friends returned home for the weekend to spend time with their family, well New York was laid back on the sofa with his girlfriend and their kids. He decided he would visit a social media to visit old friends when he stumbled upon an old girl friend of his who he had not seen in about 18 years shortly after high school.

New York was ok with seeing his old girlfriend after all he was happily in a new relationship with his new girlfriend Tausha. Well he recognized his past girl-friend's son on the social media website but what he could not make out was who was the younger boy standing beside Julia his ex-girlfriend's son on the picture who resembled him a great deal.

The little boy was small on the picture but in real life, he would now be about eighteen years old. New York went into a daze for a minute because the little boy on the picture looked exactly like him, he said to himself, "This doesn't mean anything because children sometimes look like people who are not their father." However, this did disturb him because the little boy on the picture was about eight years old and he had facial features that only New York could have known about. N.Y. knew something was wrong when the little boy he saw in the portrait even had his dental match. His teeth were identical to the boy on the picture.

Even though he suspected this boy to be his, he showed the picture to his new girl Tausha and she asked him. "Why was he looking for his ex-girlfriend Julia anyway?" He said I was not looking for Julia, I was looking to see how her son Brandon was doing after all these years and I saw a little boy standing by her son who looks just like me. "Well what do you think?" She replied, "Well it was all before my time but yes I can see a strong resemblance of you in the kid?" She also told him. "Have you seen a picture of him recent at the age of 18?' New York said, "Yes, I have."

He showed the picture to his new girlfriend Tausha who immediately said, "This child is your twin but if you reach out to him he may have another father or you may have to pay back child support."

"I will not stop you from looking for your kid instead I will support you." New York began looking for his child on social media, He in boxed his ex-girlfriend Julia on social media, she realized that New York had found out about the child after all these years.

In fact, she had giving him another father who was not there at the time maybe he figured out the child was not his and just left the situation. Julia saw the inbox from N.Y. asking about whether the kid standing beside her son Brandon on the old picture was his or not but she did not answer for at least a whole year.

The boy's mother Julia was afraid what would happen now once her son found out that she gave him the wrong father. There were many questions that needed to be addressed, like did you do it out of anger to hurt his daddy or did she do it on purpose. Julia just could not speak at this time because she knew she had hurt her son, whose name was Zion because she gave him the wrong father.

It was hard for N.Y. because now he really didn't know if the child in question was his or not especially without cooperation from the mother. Well the mother had a great deal to lose, it was possible that her son would not like her if she told him he had another father. Many problems had to be worked out. Another problem with the situation with the child being the age of 18, he could not depend on himself. He still needed a roof over his head provided by the mother.

In addition to these problems, the son relied solely on the mother's help still. Well as time progressed it took a lot out of New York, he couldn't even rest well at night knowing he had another child out there that was basically his twin. N.Y. never met the boy but once he saw that he and his son were identical to each other, this automatically created a bond that would last forever.

The depressed father was still going to work and still being a great father to his own two kids at home but he never was emotionally or mentally stable, he was a mental time bomb ticking away that the eyes could not see.

His close friend Mississippi knew everything about him and finally approached his friend and asked him what was wrong with him. New York shrugged it off at first because he didn't want to talk about it. Sip told him. "I know something is wrong because you are not the person you use to be." "I believe you are on drugs." I am not on drugs, he replied. "Ok, I will tell you what it is, partner recently I found out that I have an eighteen-year-old identical son that I knew nothing at all about." "You mean to tell me that you have an eighteen-year-old son that you knew nothing about?"

"Well let me ask you this, how you knew nothing about him" "I mean you had to know something about him." Every year thousands of men in America do not claim their kids and this leaves them to become young kids with hate in their hearts. N.Y. launched a search for his long lost son because he lost his own father at the age of three years old therefore he can relate to the pain that a kids goes through without having a father in his life. New York was also a public speaker for the youth, he had already spoken to students at Universities, boys and girl's clubs.

He remembered when he had to face the small children in elementary class when he lost his father at three years old. It was easy to exchange a pencil or paper or even share a lunch together but it is irreplaceable to replace a father.

The problem nowadays with some mothers and fathers they believe that their kids are made of material instead of real people. We should not treat kids or teens as if they are a doll or something in a fantasy world when they are real people with real feelings.

New York remembered the pain he had to deal with, he wasn't mad or jealous with losing his father at the young age of three. He made the worst of a bad situation, even though he lost his father at the age of three he gained his friends father's love and attention. N.Y. rode in the truck with his friends' father.

His friends didn't mind sharing their father with New York as a little boy once he lost his father at an early age. N. Y. remembered while losing his father at such a young age of three. He recalled father jokes were the worst. Another thing he was dramatized by as a little boy was he didn't have a father around to give him money so he didn't have the finest things that his friends at school had.

It is a big difference when two people are raising a child because it literally takes two people to raise a child because it is a very hard job to raise a child some people think it takes a village to raise a child. Another significant difference is the income will be greater with two parents but N.Y. Mother was a strong woman and raised him without a father.

Although he had a step father who came into his mother's life when he was a grown up, many people don't know it but a really good step-father can make a big difference in a kid's life if he shows them time and love. Even though New York had no lead on his long lost son who he discovered he had living without his knowledge up until now.

Even though he had no bond with the son he had never seen, he didn't want to leave or abandon his son like he felt he was abandoned. See he was a young child when they buried his own father and couldn't understand why death couldn't be recalled. He did not know anything about death, an explanation of death makes no sense to a hurting man. Every kid in the world need someone to love them no matter if they are children or teens.

I suggest that we try to love someone today and give them something they need in their life. Let me ask you, have you did anything good for anyone today? If not whatever you give to someone, it will come back good to you and every time you do a bad deed, it will come back to you to.

New York was a nice white guy not that his race really mattered but it is rare to see such a young person at the age of 34 administering to the care of a child on or off the street. It didn't matter to N.Y. if a child was struggling in the classroom or if he saw him struggling in the street and he didn't get paid for it.

It was not about the money to N.Y. he really cared about the children and he was a good Christin. He visited many churches and gave what he could to homeless people. He believed that the church was in his heart and when he gave people money, he saw on the street he wasn't looking for the money back but somehow some way when he wasn't expecting his money back God gave him a blessing he didn't have room to receive. There were teens holding big machine guns on the street but they would stop and smile at N.Y. with respect because he could reach them and care for them.

It was like God sent N.Y. here on this earth now

he was not the perfect man but he would be the first to help out in most cases he emptied his pocket out to the homeless in need. He was homeless himself, he had to live in a shelter at least three times in his life and he was adamant about helping people.

Maybe God made him this way because God knew he had to have passion to receive his long lost son, he could not receive him if God had not made him passionate for kids. He hated to see anybody doing anything to harm anyone especially kids. It was a shame for him to go through life not knowing his own son and he cared about everyone else cares and hurts. There were no leads on being connected with his long lost son at least not right now but with the heart and love that N.Y. had he would wait his whole lifetime on

getting his son.

CHp 3. New York & Mississippi Visits Webb M.S.

The Temp service was going great for the guys and the economy was booming but there was a severe epidemic that were trending with the pair children at the local high school. It was the third time that a school shooting occurred at the school also drugs were being brought into the school, which made it easy for their children to be exposed to drugs.

The duo raised their children close which meant they went to the same high school together. Sip and New York were called to New York High School to watch a video of a clip where their two children were on camera smoking a marijuana cigarette in the hallways once the main principal was not at work. The camera also showed their two girls entering the men bathroom at the school and coming out at least ten minutes late. The bathroom didn't have camera in it but you can just imagine what was going on inside this restroom.

It was too much drama especially when you know how a father is over jealous about his little girls. Mississippi daughter was now thirteen and became pregnant with the high school principal baby.

Sippi was another nickname for Mississippi, he became furious and wanted to go to the school to hurt the principal at New York High but he remembered what happened when he got in trouble for entering the couple's house without an invitation and almost did twenty-five to life. He kept a handgun on him at all times which he named Susie. Sip knew he had to do something to change the direction of his daughter's Amanda's faith, she was already pregnant by the high school principal at the age of thirteen. He finished his shift at the temporary agency at the end of the day and reported to his boss.

He told the boss that it was emergency that he leaves the state of New York before he catches a case and end up doing life almost as the same situation earlier as when he landed in jail before. His boss asked Mississippi, "Would a raise change his mind about staying and working for the temp?"

Sippi told him, "I know you will miss me, I am a very hard worker from Greenville M.S. I made you a lot of money and I don't want to hurt you." "My daughter is in trouble and there is not enough money in the world that could change the way I feel about my daughter and her safety." The boss replied, "Well I should have known I couldn't keep you forever, I appreciate everything you have did for the Temp and as long as you put in your two weeks' notice I will give you money for traveling expenses." Sip grabbed his boss who was white not that this mattered but he embraced him.

His employer told him, "I hate to see you go but I hate to see you unhappy." Sip told him He loved him and the boss immediately replied he loved him back. The two-week's notice was set in place and so was Sippi's trip to Webb M.S.

The only thing left to do now was return to the high school where his daughter was attending and turn in her books. Upon his arrival to the school, he saw his buddy N.Y. who made a visit to the school also. He asked his buddy, "Why was he at New York High today?" His friend replied to him, "I had to come to the school today again because I have received complaints from the teachers here about my kids." N.Y. told Sip,

"The principal has suspended his daughter indefinitely from the school and she has absolutely no school to go to in the middle of the 3rd semester." "Why are you at the school yourself?" "I came here to turn in my daughter's books to the school because I have received several complaints about my daughter

Amanda too."

New York explained to sip now he doesn't have another school available to enroll his daughter in during the middle of the 3rd semester.

His partner explained to him, "I am moving to this town in M.S. called Webb M.S." It is a very small town but I believe this is what our children needs right now a very small town maybe they can fit in down there with the other students because life won't be so fast. Well, replied N.Y. replied, "Do you think I can get my kids into the School because I don't want them to fall behind." I believe life in a small town called Webb Mississippi may not be bad at all.

The following week the pair loaded up both their small families on three trucks and proceeded out of town in the middle of the night heading down south to Webb M.S. They arrived in Webb Mississippi during sunrise in the morning but once the fog went away, daylight finally appeared.

The two guys were amazed to see there were very little stores in the town. They realized they came to the very small town of Webb to enroll their children in the high school. New York and Sip purchased two brick houses on the outstretch of Webb, it was a subdivision called Goose pond.

It was a subdivision, which consisted of three streets, but it was a large complex. Sip lived on the 2nd street near the highway and N.Y. lived on the 1st street. Everyone was all settled in and moved into their houses when all of a sudden Sip saw a guy he knew from New York City, it was his old friend Dollar Bob. "He asked him how long have you been in Webb M.S.?" Dollar Bob was clean he wore a three-piece suit every day and he was quite the ladies' man.

He had three women with him at the time. Dollar Bob replied, "I have been in Webb now for ten years and I like it here." "The police don't harass you down here, they let us mind our business and they also mind theirs." "What bring you here to Webb M.S. Dollar Bob asked?" "Well my children were acting up in school and it was finally the last straw for them." "I relocated them to a safer place with a local high school."

"Well the school is right over on highway 49." I also relocated here with my friend New York." Dollar

Bob replied, "Yes there is a white guy who moved in the vacant house beside me on the 1st street." "Yes that is my friend, we moved here yesterday."

Early the next morning the two guys enrolled their two daughters at the local high school in Webb M.S. Sip and N.Y. once they enrolled their daughters in school here, the parents had to find some work. I mean their past boss at the temporary office back in New York had given them money for transportation and to relocate but it was running out very fast.

The two parents wondered how they could make a living in Webb M.S. with the stores burned down they had very little resources. The idea hit the guys, they proposed a legislature idea to the mayor of Webb Mr. Livingston at the time.

The proposal read that Mississippi whose real name was Michael Jones and New York whose real name was Diablo Jenkins would sign the contract to build the stores back in Webb M.S. The Mayor of Webb had applied for the grant to rebuild the stores and pay the workers who built the stores.

The guys were familiar with driving a crane which paid 35 dollars per hour also they were very skilled in laying sheet rock. The two dudes made friends with the other young guys in Webb and offered them a job as well. Dollar Bob drove passed the post office in Webb and was glad to see the guys reconstructing the first store on the corner.

Dollar Bob got out of his Cadillac, he went over to the work site. Immediately he shook his two new friend's hands and told them, "He was glad to see them get employment to raise their family."

He also told them, "You are doing the town of Webb M.S. Tallahatchie County a great community deed to fix these buildings." Dollar Bob was wearing a mink coat, he didn't have to work he had five women in his entourage everywhere he went. Sometimes he danced in the town on the streets to entertain the people, everyone knew Dollar Bob.

In no time with the two entrepreneur's business was booming, the two started rebuilding the town also the youth was employed in the reconstruction of Webb Mississippi. The guys worked hard, they wore yellow hard hats. Very shortly, the store on the corner was built very quickly and the people could shop in the store.

Once again, the citizens of Webb had a brand new store to buy produce, food, and personal items. The name of this store was called Food's General and it was filled with people every day.

Even though the town had finally received another grocery store there were more stores to be rebuilt because New York and Sip still had some time left on the contract. Once the job was done, the workers met with their Boss of the construction site. Mr. Goston congratulated the workers for completing Food General, he also explained to the gentlemen that the next building they were going to build was a clothing store.

The workers received their check for the day

and returned home so they could start working on the clothing store Monday morning. In the meanwhile, the friends held a barbecue in Goosepond to get to know the neighbors a little better. Well, all the brick houses were built very close together in the neighborhood. The new neighbors played loud music on the 1st street.

An old neighbor came buy and chilled with New York and Sip. His name was Mr. Groovy, he told them about all the years he lived in Goosepond. He informed the guys, "They were lucky to come from New York and get a job, the only jobs we had had was working in the fields chopping cotton." He added, "There were a few factory jobs in Tutwiler M.S. but for the most part there were not any jobs in Webb." New

York asked Groovy, "What was it like to chop cotton?"

Well groovy explained to him, "You better knew what you were doing because if you made a mistake and chopped the cotton the black straw boss would act a fool worse than the white owner did."

N.Y. who was from New York didn't know anything about chopping cotton but his friend Sip did because he was from Greenville Mississippi. N.Y. said, "I thought it was called chopping cotton!" Dollar Bob who was next door standing next to his Cadillac and wearing fifteen gold chains also chimed in on the conversation. He told N.Y. "One time the black boss kicked him because he chopped down a stalk of cotton and told him to walk home the best way he could in the extremely hot sun." Dollar Bob also told him that the boss who drove the workers to the field were called hands or hoe hands. He said, "He himself was driving workers to the field and at the end of the day the boss told him to go pay off all the hands and bring my truck back."

"When you made it to the end of your row of cotton, there were water waiting on you to drink but if you got smart or said anything to the boss you were fired on the spot." The music was playing loud on the 1st street in Goospond everyone was eating food and having fun. Dollar Bob left with all his women and went up town to sit in front of the laundromat, which was called the washer. There were many people standing in front of the washer in Webb, it was a way to meet and greet people you have not seen in a while.

Meanwhile back in Goosepond the stories of the legendry brick subdivision were being told.

A very old resident name Jimmy came through on a walker, he joined in on the conversation and said, "I remember when there was no asphalt on these streets, there were only red dirt and water everywhere." "The water here was very rusty looking until we went to Jackson and stood up for our civil rights to have good drinking water to drink and wash in 1982."

"I moved here in 1973 when there were only a few houses here, the only houses here were the ones built on the back street which was called 3rd street." Everyone gathered around the barbecue event held on the 1st street with New York and Sip and chimed in on all the good times shared in Goosepond and there were many stories to tell. When the Elder man Mr. Jimmy finished speaking at the barbecue on 1st street another resident about 53 spoke his mind on living in Goosepond. His name was Mr. Kool he said, "All these streets 1st, 2nd and 3rd are all united now."

He continued to speak, "In the 80's if you were caught on a different street you would most definitely have to fight." "The candy store was on the 1st street if you were caught on the 1st street trying to go over Mr. Sandy's house to get some hot balls, lemon heads, Charleston chews and other candy you would get jumped on. "If you knew your short cuts, you could run through somebody's yard and get away." "If you didn't know any shortcuts you would get caught and pay the price until you learn to stay off 1st street."

The basketball goal was on the third street, it was ok to play basketball until someone got mad because they lost their game. A fight often broke out many times and I remember there were gunshots fired often because someone was playing dirty basketball.

The basketball goal was a way for residents to improve their skills when they played for the Jr high, high school or even college ball. There were good times at the basketball goal everyday wasn't a bad day but you better know who you were speaking with because some of the resident in Goosepond were friendly but basketball can bring out the anger in a friend.

Now at the barbecue was a resident named Kool.

He said, "Another way we made money in Goosepond was walking the roads every day collecting aluminum cans." "If you filled up a one- hundred-pound sack, you could earn at least forty-dollars for spending change to have in your pockets." "You could take the cans to the town of Webb and cash in your cans as long as no mud was found stomped in your cans."

"Some people put mud in their cans to make the cans weigh more hoping it would increase their pay." "If you were found with mud stomped in your cans, you would be embarrassed and told not to come back again and everybody laughed at you." New York was laughing at the barbecue because he was from New York but Sip already knew about life in Mississippi. Let me put my two cents in said another guy who was just passing through on 1st street.

"You could go to the pecan orchard by the bridge in Webb and pick up pecans to make some money as long as you turned all the pecans in." "The problem was many people wanted to turn half the pecans in and keep the other half because the owner of the orchard was old and couldn't see but he had a younger son that would catch you if you put a brick in your bag."

New York said while drinking on a beer, "You guys were wild, it sounds like you had a tremendous amount of fun living here in Goose pond." The barbecue was fun and the day was ending, Dollar Bob drove back home to stop for the day however he left his girls at his house and came to chill for the rest of the night at the barbecue on 1st street. Once the barbecue was over everyone went home. New York noticed someone was stealing his children clothes off the clothesline outside. Whoever was stealing the clothes off the clothesline at dark managed to get away with all of New York daughter's clothes.

Now she had to miss a day of school in Webb, she had to get new things from the department store so they took her to a larger town nearby called Clarksdale M.S. Clarksdale had more stores and way more businesses than Webb. N.Y. daughter Lyndsey noticed how large Clarksdale was. She said, "Dad this town is almost like New York City." N.Y. said, "Well it is large and nice but it is not as big as N.Y. but I like it and I will bring you and C.J. back to visit." "Look dad it has a bowling alley," she said. "Yes daughter, I like Clarksdale and we will be back as soon as I get some spending money." Lyndsey had new clothes to wear to school in Webb and they were very nice clothes. N.Y. took the 49-west exit and headed back to Webb M.S. The next day in school the English teacher Mrs. Johnson noticed the clothes and gave her a very nice compliment.

All the children loved the new school in Webb, even Sip's daughter Amanda who was in the 10th grade joined the basketball team called the lady Trojans. Amanda was all-pro and lead the school to a 2a championship in basketball. She received the trophy for most improved player and MVP of the year.

When they won the state Championship in

Jackson M.S. the town of Webb prepared for a parade through the town. The next day all the basketball team was dress up, they were riding on a float down through Webb M.S. The students of the school threw candy at the citizens of Webb M.S. There were very nice cars and even old classics cars in the parade in the town of Webb. Everyone was having a good time.

The fun was extended another day in Webb because it was the town's tradition day also known as Webb day. Now Webb day consisted of people who had moved away to other states in northern areas often came back to see everyone who they have not seen. There were motorcycles, loud music being played. Venues cooked plenty of food and everyone was eating and enjoying themselves. Once again

Dollar Bob put on a dancing show at Webb day on the streets, everyone enjoyed seeing him dance he was a dancer from the old school. He was always laughing with a distinct smile on his face and he didn't bother no one. Every time you saw Dollar Bob he was full of cheer.

The town of Webb made a lot of money on Webb Day and people from miles around came to see. The news center came to visit the historical event and featured the excitement in the evening news on channel t.v. 6. It was a joyful event, even though the town was small the citizens were large in heart.

The town citizens cleaned up everything and began to resume the town as usual the next day. They will never forget the wonderful times shared on Webb day and they looked forward to hosting the event next year.

The town resumed back to normal the next business day, the kids went to Webb High School and the parents went back to work on repairing and rebuilding the stores to the town. The construction workers were working on building a clothing store, which was almost completed in the town. Rebuilding the town will not take long because New York and Mississippi hired some of the citizens of Webb to help them rebuild so everything was taking shape at a great velocity of speed.

Finally, the clothing store was built once they had the electrician to installed the electricity and have the inspection come out to check everything to see if inspection passed, everyone was able to shop in the store. The clothing stores was called Jay's fashion, it had a wide variety of woman, men, boys, and girl's clothing. Now the entire workers were paid for the job and they could now take a long needed break after working so hard.

There was a huge celebration held in Goosepond after the red ribbon was cut. During the interim of working, there was time to do a little freelancing because the next building project of the town didn't start until three-weeks later.

While the pair from New York was driving along highway 49 they noticed a memorial building named after Emmet Till, this is a large recreation where the town citizens use for a repast when someone pass away or just when they rented the building. New York was surprised to see that this was near the hometown of Emmet Till.

They drove further down highway 49 until they reached the town of Sumner, they saw another venue honoring the late Mr. Till, this time they saw tour buses visiting from around the world to see the museum of the late Mr. Emmet and New York was impressed also Sip because the monument was not there when he left Mississippi.

The New Yorkers was now traveling through Sumner Mississippi just enjoying the historical sites. Once the friends left the historical history sites, they went finishing in a lake called Cassidy bayou located on the backroads by a country club, there were plenty fish to catch and the two did just that. New York and

Sip had enough food to cook and eat when they made it home to Goosepond. Two weeks has passed away leaving the construction workers only one week to relax. The town of Webb is now starting to take shape.

It is beginning to look full now with the spaces from the burned down building being replaced. Well finally, Monday morning came and the construction crew retuned to Webb to build another building in the vacant space. The workers were being paid twenty-five dollars per hour to rebuild the town of Webb.

The construction begins, as normal day in and day out was the same pattern. Going to work and getting off was the usual routine. The construction site consisted of cranes, sheet rock, bulldozers and other farm equipment. The workers wore hard hats, the construction site was taped off with yellow tape so no one who was not working could enter or get hurt. It was now 12 noon on a busy day of construction in Webb and the workers are hungry. The popular place in Webb was called the burger joint located on the side near the car wash. Everyone loved the burger joint because they served good hamburgers and good food.

The entire construction crew walked over to the burger joint and bought food. They were now building an Appliance store, which sold washing machines, bicycles, stoves, and refrigerators. The owner of this appliance store was so friendly, he would let you put the appliances on your credit account without even really knowing you. He had some guys working for him that would load the truck and bring it right to your house with no problem as long as you paid him.

The storeowner of the appliance store was very nice, he didn't care what house hold member paid him as long as somebody paid him some money this is how credit was explained in Webb M.S. If you paid your bills on time in Webb, you could always get something else. The town was small but business remained the same. Business remained the same in Mississippi as well as it did in New York.

It cost money to live in a large city or a very small town, nothing has changed about money and I don't believe nothing will ever change about a dollar bill. In the urban society, there is an old phrase. "Get it how you live." If you live scandalous then get what you need in a scandalous way, which won't lead to a good end. If you get it in an honest way, you will survive. There were once an old neighbor of mines living in Goosepond. She explained to me as a little boy growing up about ten tears old she said, "Everything that you do or make, do it with your hands." I understood immediately as a little boy what she was telling me.

Nowadays the youth don't understand the value of a hard working dollar because everything has been handed to them and they still believe someone owes them something. If you are from Webbs M.S. or New York City the hustle is still the same, no one is a smart as the other as long as the survival is still the same. Another hustle is called the turn, if you have something to bring to the table and sale you can put it on the turn and sale.

No matter where you are, a large city or small town people are still the same because people are the same wherever you go. No one is as smart another person. This is what get most people caught up trying to rip someone off because they thought no one was smart enough to figure out their fraud. When you think you are the smartest one this is when you lose the game the hustle.

Someone always have their eyes on you and suspect you for your sinister ways or scandalous moves, they do not have to tell you they are watching you but they are at all times. Whether in N.Y. or M.S. the hustle was still the same and this was how to survive. You had better believe in God, he is in charge and money exchange hands equally in society this is all that really mattered. If you don't have a hustle then you don't fit in this urban society, so then you have the option of going to jail or prison or even the grave. You can either sink or swim in this urban society. You will weed and seed your own self out of this urban community where you don't belong.

You will hurt your own self in this society trying to live your life without achieving things with your hand and trying to find a slicker clever route. If you don't achieve anything you want in life honestly you will fail every time so it didn't really matter what city or town you are from, the survival game is still the same.

Things was going great in Webb M.S. the gang have lived nearly four years in the wonderful small town. The whole town was now completed with stores. Everything worked out perfectly, the citizens of Webb were employed for four years and now owned houses in the town. The children have now graduated from Webb High School. Amanda received and basketball scholarship to play at a four-year university. Lyndsey and C.J. completed school now and received an academic scholarship to a four-year University.

Well everything has taken shape the town was beautiful with brand new stores. New York and Sip was comfortably living with their houses in Goosepond but they were struggling on unemployment because the job had ended.

It was hard for them to pay their utilities now with the gas prices going way up. Their unemployment was about to expire in one months and there were questions about how the two families would survive without unemployment benefits. There was no question about it, there was no way the children could go to college if they depended on their fathers to pay for the expenses. Surely all three of the children received scholarships but without any income coming in they could not afford the basic necessities a child needed to attend college.

The family had to put their head together after living a four-year stint in Webb M.S, suddenly it hit the two providers they had to leave M.S. really they had no choice because their insurance benefits were set to expire. New York made a phone call to their old boss in N.Y. to see if he could get his old job back however when he called the old job phone number the recording said, "This number is no longer in service."

Sip tried to google the temp agency on the internet and his findings were this place of business is closed down to the spread of covid 19. The family had to do something with the expiring of their unemployment benefits was approaching very rapidly. New York and Sip had a hard time explaining to their children that their college careers may have to wait or be postponed.

All of a sudden New York received a disturbing phone call from his niece in N.Y. stating that his grandfather passed away peacefully in his sleep. It was painful news for N.Y. considering he loved his grandfather so much.

There was a silver lining to this bad news, Cynthia his niece informed him that his grandfather left N.Y. some money but it is not known how much. He explained to his niece, can you tell me how much money grandfather left because I don't even have a job now and my benefits are about to run out. His niece read the will aloud to her uncle and the will read that New York was the recipient of $100,000 dollars left by his grandfather in the will. The money was available as soon as the insurance company received the signature from the beneficiary holder.

N.Y. called the insurance company on the telephone and Mrs. Nancy reassured him that once he returns to the state of New York he could receive all of his benefits on the spot. He then informed Sip of the bad news of his father passing away in his sleep.

Sip offered his condolences, immediately he informed Mississippi of his father leaving him $100,000 dollars that is available upon on receipt of his signature. Sip hugged his partner and said, this is good news for you partner considering your situation with the unemployment benefits elapsing. "What are you doing with your inheritance said his buddy?" "Well I was thinking about relocating back to New York." "We have raised our Children in a safe town of Webb M.S. also we have restored the towns stores to 100%." "You heard all the natives in Webb say that we were lucky to find employment here in Webb." "I am heading back to New York City, it looks like the only option." I will miss you dearly said Sip. "Well I was thinking about taking you back to New York with me buddy." "I believe I can loan you the money to get your own apartment until you get on your feet." Mississippi said, "You are the greatest partner anyone could have been blessed to have."

The plans had been made for the northerners to go back to N.Y. so they scheduled one last barbecue on 1st street the day before they left the town of Webb. Once again like before everyone came over on the 1st street to pay farewell to the guys plus relive the good times in the small town.

Now N.Y. had some memories he shared in Webb. He opened up with the time someone stole his daughter's clothes off the clothesline. Well of course, the town's dancer Dollar Bob was there to see the family off to New York also to speak about old times in Goosepond.

The guys really had the subdivision smoking with barbecue smoke and loud music and some people showed up to eat a free meal.

There were so many people at the barbecue thanking the guys for rebuilding the stores of Webb and revising the economy to the town residents. The construction workers who was employed to help build the stores came out to attend the barbecue and was reminiscing about old times they shared rebuilding the stores in Webb. New York and Sip created a bond with the community of Webb and Goosepond so great that the community did not want them to leave.

The barbecue party lasted all night because the travelers were packed and ready to leave for New York first thing in the morning. The alarm clock rang at 10:00 am Monday morning this was the sign for everyone to gather all their remaining clothing and head for the trucks that was parked outside. There were no times to waste their goodbyes had already been said at the barbecue. The family truck was loaded up and they were headed back to New York. Sip along with N.Y. made a stop at Webb store on highway 49 to fill up with gas and to get a snack.

When ironically they saw the town Mayor Mr. Livingston also getting gas. He asked the guys, "Where were the going?" They each responded, "We are headed back to New York City." Mr. Livingston the mayor of the town of Webb thanked the guys and handed them each an extra three-hundred dollars for their trip and hugged both of them for rebuilding the stores of the small town.

He explained to both of the men if they ever needed a job in Webb they were more than welcome to call him on his cell phone. He handed them his number to his private cell phone and told the guys to call them whenever they wanted to talk. "Mr. Livingston said, "I am going to let you guys get going now but the business in this town is booming now thanks to both of you splendid men God bless you."

Immediately after pumping gas the family headed highway 49 west to Clarksdale M.S. until they reached highway 61 heading to Memphis Tennessee.

Chp. 4. New York And Mississippi moves back to N.Y.

While traveling on the road for approximately twelve hours the family could finally see the Statue of Liberty standing in the New York Harbor it was definitely a sure and a reality sign they were back home in New York. Once they made it into the town of New York, the settlers had to find a realtor because they really didn't have time to find a place to live.

About three hours later New York received a call on his cell phone inquiring about a property in Manhattan. A property realtor offered a nice luxurious mansion sitting on four-hundred acres of land. This house had a gardener who took care of the pretty flowers every day. The flower arrangement in the yard were lovely with assorted color roses. There were purple flowers, red roses, yellow dandelions and all kind of plant you could think of.

There was a lake in the back of the mansion. The property realtors finalized the deal and now New York was the proud owner of a mansion sitting on four-hundred acres' land in Manhattan N.Y.

The grass was cut nice and even, it was most definitely a nice place to play golf. There were no neighbors to complain about anything. The new house was located on a dead end street with no one living next to the house. In the meanwhile, it took Mississippi a whole week to get a call from a property realtor. Finally, Mrs. Williams the property manager from Robert property called and proposed the idea of a nice four-bed room house. It was not as big as New York's house but at least now he could move his family out of the hotel. The deal was finalized but in such a short time, the movers had to take what was offered.

Mississippi's new four bedroom apartments was located in Queens N.Y. The families were all settled in New York and was ready to resume a new life. It was a new life in New York for both of the parents. I mean thing were different this time around. The kids were all grown up now and ready to attend college in a month. Even though N.Y. and Sip was living in two places in New York, they would call each other every day. The guys were back in the big apple. Well Mississippi knew what skills he needed to survive after being a construction worker in Webb M.S. Sip immediately went to work in Queens N.Y. with Tanden Construction L.L.C. Sip was very skilled in using the bobcat to move debris.

He was an all-around worker and could be used in any position. Well New York did not immediately need a job after all, he paid his mansion off and didn't owe a mortgage. Sure, he had expenses but he had more time to waste than Sippi did. Tanden Construction consisted of many workers.

Every day at the construction site day in and day out was the same. The workers at the job wore hard hats, disused politics, and family life. One day a young white teenager at the job was talking about his family situation. He said, "He didn't know his dad until last year." He also said, "The man who he was told his daddy was not his real father." The boy further said, "I really didn't believe the story my mom told me about another guy was my father because he didn't look like me." "I became furious with my mom for lying to me all these years but what can I do, she is still my mom right." The boy who was filled with emotions told sip, "I found out when I overheard my mom tell a friend on the phone that my real father was looking for me."

"He found out that he had a son after sixteen years." "I am 18 years old now and capable of making up my own mind who I want in my life." "Well," said Mississippi have you began looking for your father?" "I don't know where to start?" "Do you at least know his name?" asked Sip. "Yes I know his real name said the youngster." Sip told him to search the internet."

While searching the internet the kid found something interesting on his first search. The internet listed that his father who he had never seen in life was a construction worker and his last employer was from a construction job in Webb M.S. Sip asked the teenager, "You must be joking?" "I would most definitely not be joking about finding my father sir."

The boy noticed that once Sippi heard him, he began staring and looking at the young boy's face and he could not believe what he was thinking, he could not say a word. Break time was almost over and it was time to go back to work when suddenly Sip grabbed the little boy and told him, "I have someone I think you should meet." When work was over the two workers waited outside the construction plant and sat on the benches. Mississippi reached into his pocket to get his cell phone to call New York.

Once N.Y. answered Sip put the phone on speakerphone, he told New York, "I think I have someone you should talk to. "Well go ahead," Said New York. The teenager began asking his long lost father a lot of questions, which New York confirmed to be true his long lost son. New York screamed, "Finally God has heard my prayers and reunited me with my son." There was joy in his long lost son's heart to be reunited with his father after eighteen long years.

The long lost father and son exchanged numbers, address and stayed in touch with each other. When New York hung up the phone with his son, he thanked his pal for being nice to him and reuniting him with his son. N.Y. also told Sip, "Remember early when I told you that you owed me?" "Well you have paid the price and don't owe me nothing not even the money I loaned you to purchase your apartment here in New York." There is no price on friendship and I am glad to have you in my life. "Likewise, Said Sip "You have always been there for me buddy consider it no problem at all.

Mississippi remembered when he was locked in jail facing a life sentence when his old friend N.Y pulled some strings from a fake attorney who was an unlicensed practicing lawyer however, the lawyer was able to free his buddy Mississippi from life in prison.

The two guys needed each other, it wasn't time for racism because there is an old saying called fair exchange is no robbery. New York needed Mississippi in the black community and Mississippi needed New York in the white urban community. If you have something to bring to the bargaining table, it has to be equal.

There was no time for racism especially when the color of money was green. Sure, there are prejudice people in this world but these people don't not live in an urban society. There were all kind of races in New York in this urban community trying to live together. In The Bronx New York in the poor community living together in a large house.

New York recalled as a youngster living in the

Bronx N.Y. in 1973. No matter what race you were you had to stick together to survive. It was a big old house in the Bronx, the electricity was turned on in someone else's name. He recalled the residents ran an electric cord down to the second floor to an electric outlet cord, this is how the whole house had electricity. In this large house in the Bronx, there was a food pantry nearby.

The community gathered food from the pantry and the food was cooked and shared with everyone in the house. There was no time for racism when everyone was Poor. Even though there were no jobs in this community in the Bronx, in 1973 the neighborhood had a black author living in the hood. Some of the residents were fired from their jobs and denied unemployment especially from temporary agencies. Well this black author was a good writer. He would write a letter for the people in the poor areas of the Bronx. A letter was written to the unemployment office to request an appeal for the workers fired by agencies that wouldn't pay money to residents. The author wrote several appeals letters to the unemployment office for black and whites who was denied unemployment benefits.

He was successful at winning the unemployment appeals and the residents was paid their money benefits from the unemployment office. Once in 1973 while living in the old house, the tenants faced eviction and relied on the black author again. Author Williams contacted a legal aid lawyer at no cost to him.

Author told the lawyer about how the past property owners took over and raised the rent in the Bronx N.Y. It was already nearly impossible to pay the rent before they received the increase in the rent. Court began downtown at city hall at 8 am to evict thirty-people living in this two-story building. The property realtors showed up on time in court as well as the 30 tenants fighting to stop an eviction. Author Williams showed up with his legal aid lawyer to fight against one of New York finest attorney, she represented the property managers.

The top hired lawyer was sure she would win her case against Author Williams and the legal aid lawyer representing 30 clients ready to face homelessness out into the streets. N.Y. remembered growing up as a little kid in the Bronx in 1973 it was very cold that year and it would have been devastating to face eviction out into the cold. The top firm attorney presented her case for the building agency. She said, "The tenants in the building haven't paid any money to the rent realtor and they have to be evicted in 10 days. Author Williams and his legal aid lawyer took the stand and their defense was, "The landlords raised the rent without fixing any of their property and the rent was just too high."

The court deliberated after hearing both arguments. The judge called a recess then later issued a verdict. The verdict was in favor of Author Williams and the appointed free legal aid lawyer, together they had defeated the top Lawyer in whole New York City.

The Lawyer name was Attorney Whitney, she couldn't stand to be beaten by an Author and a legal aid lawyer so she appealed the case and she was beaten one more time by the Author and legal aid lawyer. Finally, on the third appeal she was able to beat the Author and legal aid lawyer and all 30 tenants was evicted but since they won two months appeals it was summer time and hot outside when they finally got evicted. New York recalled this in 1973 in the Bronx New York while trying to survive there as a youngster.

What I am trying to paint to you is, well I guess racism will always exist but if you bring racism to the table where you need everyone and everyone is hungry. You will not eat yourself. The Bronx has very beautiful luxury places in it also. There were beautiful places in the Bronx New York even today. There is

luxurious mansion with swimming pools in the back.

There is a completely industrial court filled with

businesses in the Bronx New York Today.

CH 5   Betrayal Is Dangerous

It was a typical day in Queens New York, well N.Y and Sip was firm believers in God but they did make mistakes. The two didn't not use hard drugs but they did use marijuana just to relax from a hard day's work. Mississippi rode his convertible 1983 Mercedes down the street to purchase cannibal from a well-known friend who was well trusted.

The drop was made and sip was on his way back home. To relax and chill for the rest of the day when all of a sudden he was pulled over by the cops with guns drawn to his head. "Don't move said one cop or I will shoot." Well Mississippi was familiar with the city. He knew when the cops pull you over to keep your hands visible at all time so he put his hands in the air and quietly said, "What is the problem Officer?" The dispatch said on the radio. "We have caught the serial killer, the one who has raped 10 women finally." Sip heard this on the radio and his jaws dropped but he didn't resist arrest because resisting arrest is a felony in most states now.

The police showed Mississippi a picture of a person who looked just like him. Sip began to say, "There has to be some mistake officer." "I work a job every day and is a law abiding citizen." This made the African American officer very angry and he told Sip, "To shut up before I blow you away and feel no remorse for it." "Where you are going the fellows are

100

going to love you." Even though Mississippi was traumatized, he couldn't help but to noticed the guy on the police mugshot picture looked exactly like him. Sip told the police, "African Americans look alike to white people."

This was the final draw when the black police officer struck him in the head with his flashlight because some of the woman who were abused were African American little girls. Since some of the teenagers were abducted, they asked the suspect where are these women and teenaged girls. Most definitely, a serial killer was on the loose.

It was a terrible misunderstanding that could not be proven at this point because when they booked Sip he had the same fingerprints and dna as the serial killer. He was booked again at New York headquarters precinct, this time he was registered as a sex offender. His picture was taken and he made the evening news at 6pm also again at 10pm. His friend N.Y. was watering his flowers when he saw Sip's face on the evening news and was devastated.

The news center then showed the real serial killer, abductor and rapist. New York was sure it was his partner Sip because there was no difference in the picture. The pressure was on Sippi because he didn't know where the ladies who were abducted and raped was located. He had absolutely no idea what was happening to him.

However, at the N.Y. precinct he had to call his only friend New York. When N.Y. saw the phone call coming in from the police station, he did not answer Sip's call. All the information added up on his friend. The N.Y. newspaper read the killer was born in a hospital in Greenville M.S. N.Y. knew that sip was born in Greenville M.S. New York said to himself. "Let him rot in jail because it sure is him."

"I can't believe my buddy who I trusted around my own kids is a pedophile, he could have very well done the same to my kids." "I can't trust him now or help him, he is on his own now." The idea was becoming very plain to Sip that his best friend N.Y. had betrayed him.

Well the inmate only choice now was to obtain a court appointed lawyer because now at this point he had no friends at all. Right after yard call and shower call at the jail, he used the pay phone that rolled around to each individual guys in the cell. The only family he had now was in Greenville M.S. A loyal aunt who had also seen the evening news on channel 6. Once his Aunt saw the phone call coming in from a New York precinct, she accepted all charges and immediately told him, "I am ashamed of you and the whole family is ashamed of you." "I am not helping you at all, please tell the police where these missing women are and why did you abduct and rape all these women?" Sip told his Aunt, "I know how you feel but I am not guilty of any of these crimes."

Sure I am a black man doing time." The only thing I am guilty of is being a black man and circumstances." His Aunt replied to him, "Don't start giving me this lecture about you are a black man doing time when the killer has the same dna finger prints as you." "I believe someone is out to ruin my life." "No one is out to ruin your life, you have ruin your own life and made a horrific decision for your daughter who is now in college." "Auntie I need you to do something for me." I need you to go to Greenville hospital medical records because the police are telling me that this killer and rapist has my last name and dna."

"I will go to the medical records because you are my nephew but I do not believe you." "Nephew, why don't you just pray to God and do your time because you tortured these women and still won't tell the police where some of these women are!" "I am an innocent man and I hope you see it that way. "I am guilty of my streets, my project and my flats but Auntie I am an innocent man and I hope you see just that."

Sip explained to her that medical records are public and you cannot be denied to see medical records."

"Ok I will go to the records office in the morning and you will just have to accept the findings nephew." The next morning Aunt Vivica went to the medical records office at Greenville hospital.

She was very shocked at what she saw. She saw that her sister Missy who was now deceased was administered an anesthesia drug and was unconscious at birth during giving birth to twins but she only brought one of them home. She went to her grave thinking she had only one child. Vivica made a copy of this report. The next night her nephew phoned her collect from jail, she answered the phone on the first ring. Aunt Vivica told her nephew, "Get ready for the findings, are you sitting down. "Yes I am sitting down what did you find?" "Nephew your mother gave birth to twins." "Well why would my mother who said she loved me have a twin son and would not tell me." "The medical report states your mother was given anesthesia when she had birth and only signed the birth certificate for one child which was you."

"Well nephew I am sorry I didn't believe you." "That is alright Auntie, please make copies of this report and send it to my court appointed lawyer Mrs. Johnson." Ok nephew I will, also I am praying for your release."

"Auntie you may have not believed me but at

least you did not turn your back on me and I love you for this!" "Are you kidding, I have to try to make you do the right thing nephew." "I do understand." I will fax the medical records to your court lawyer right away." I am praying for your safety in there and I hope you have a speedy trial and be released." The jail phone call said, you have twenty-seconds left remaining on this phone call. Early the next morning Aunt Vivica faxed the information the information to Mississippi's lawyer hoping it would be enough to grant her nephew's freedom.

Once his lawyer received the fax of the medical records. He released a picture of the suspect again on television to clear his client's name. The state of New York was dazed and puzzled when they saw a picture of Sip's identical twin mugshot on t.v The only difference was the twin brother was identified by a tiny scar on his face caused by a car accident however if you didn't pay attention to the scar you wouldn't have not seen it. It was obvious that the inmate the state had in custody did not commit the crime. The prisoner had to remain in jail until his hearing came. When the news center released the mugshot of the twin brother this method broke the case wide open.

The estranged twin brother was living with his wife under another birth named as Theodore Adams. He was out riding around at the time but his wife saw the t.v. evening news and secretly call the authorities on her husband.

The New York squat team was notified

immediately, the police already informed his wife to stay clear of her husband because they were going to raid the house and arrest him. Once she listened to the police advice, she pretended to fall asleep in the couple's den. Once she saw Theodore was sleep, she dialed the police and entered a special code in the phone. Once the squat team saw the code entered into the phone by the suspect's wife it was a sign to enter the house with a battering ram.

The rapist and murderer was sleep when the N.Y. squat team surprised him, they entered his door with a battering ram and a flash bang. The flash bang blinded him and they arrested the dangerous serious killer. There was no need to do a dna test because one had already been done from the women he raped and murdered because they already had his dna on file, this is how they falsely arrested his brother. A dna was obtained from him anyway because it was protocol and his twin brother could not be released if it wasn't proven in court that he did not commit these crimes. Once the sample was collected from Theodore, it was revealed that he was the real serial killer and murderer. Once again it was leaked to the new center and the evening news broadcasted they have found the serial killer and rapist.

The news reporter also revealed that the rapist was an identical twin stolen at birth from his mother in Greenville M.S. New York, Sip's longtime friend saw the evening news and said, "It really was not my friend who committed these crimes." "I turned my back on a

loyal friend but he looked just like the criminal."
Mississippi was still locked up at this time and he could not be acquitted of all charges until his court date arrived which was a month later. Once the court date arrived the jury were all set and ready to acquit Sip because he was falsely accused.

The jury unanimously voted to acquit the prisoner and he was allowed to go home immediately. once again the news media announced at 6pm and 10 pm that it was a case of an identical twin brother who committed these crimes against women and teen age girls and they also announced the release of Mississippi, who was falsely accused of the charges.

Theodore the criminal's twin brother was given life without the possibility of a chance of being paroled. He admitted he killed some of the women but some of the women and teen were found through his confessions and were released from his secret confinement and were ready to live a normal life however they had to have counseling. A private funeral was held for the ladies and teen he admitted to killing and their bodies were found just where he said their locations were. Sip was released just in time the property management foreclosed on the house he was living in while he was locked up.

The good news was his mortgage management was following the whole murder trial on the news and gave the ex-prisoner a chance to catch up on his rent. Amanda Sip's daughter was glad her father was released, she hugged him once he returned home.

On the other hand, New York his once best friend made up in his mind to visit his old friend in Queens. I guess N.Y. didn't know that sometimes people forgive and sometimes they don't or sometimes they hold a grudge for you without ever telling you about it. When the old buddy arrived to see his old friend in Queens he said, "Buddy I am sorry you had to go through this terrible ordeal, also I am very sorry I thought you were the one who committed the crimes against innocent women and children."

Sippi told him, "No problem there was no way you could tell I had an identical twin because I didn't even know I had a twin myself." "Your heart was in the right place and I can't hold it against you." The duo reminisced about old times until it became dark then

New York decided he would go home to get some rest. Everything appeared normal on the surface but Sip was like a snake now he had been hurt by his disloyal friend. He was the type of person once you hurt him by being disloyal. He would not tell you because now he can't trust you. Jealously is dangerous and betrayal or being disloyal is even worst.

The worst part about it all is N.Y. never even saw any of it coming, it was like a quiet storm. It played over and over in Sippi's mind, "My friend who said he was my friend left me in jail to rot and he storms over here expecting me to have opened arms for him." "

I am going to pay him back one day but right now I have to be strong and recover from what I have been through." The released ex-inmate had been locked up for a crime that he didn't commit. Even though he didn't commit these crimes he was in jail among criminals and now have ways of a cold hearted criminal. One thing for sure he smoked a lot more now. Every day he got up early with nothing to do because jail had taught him that. Sippi often caught himself trying to wash his clothes in the commode in the bathroom like he did in jail. He was definitely a changed man with the mindset of a prisoner.

Sometimes he tried to light his cigarette by popping wires together on an electric socket, he had most definitely became adapted to the prisoner life and ways. Revenge is more dangerous when it is bottled up, it is something like a pressure cooker when it is released all at once or opened up.

Well the more time passed by he began to gradually change back in this society but this was going to take a little time. Prison life has become a part of his dna thanks to his identical twin brother Theodore who is living the rest of his life in prison. It was very traumatizing especially spending time in jail for a crime he did not commit. Even though Sippi spent time in jail for his sinister twin, he still felt compassion for his identical brother. A lot was going on in his head but there is something twins share and this is love or forgiveness. See even though his brother was a criminal sometimes genetics cannot understand this.

The Queen resident felt compassion for his twin. He would often visit his twin brother in prison to find out many things about his identical brother. He often put money on his account in prison so he could eat. He asked his brother did he know he had an identical twin brother and his twin responded, "No I never knew I had a twin brother at all." "I never meant to hurt you, I know it don't cover the embarrassment I have cost you." "Can I call you my brother his twin asked?" "Well you are my brother said Mississippi." "Well can you tell me a little about my family?"

I never knew my mom I was raised in New York all my life by a woman name Tabitha Williams, I thought she was my real mom but later I found out she had stolen me from a hospital in Greenville Mississippi." "I never heard of a twin brother until I was arrested on these charges." I watched my step father beat up my so-called mother all night and day."

One day I opened up the door to see my mother boyfriend molest my sister at least I thought she was my sister." At least I can look at you my twin brother so I can see a side of me that isn't sinister." "Maybe if I wasn't switched at birth at that hospital maybe I would be as successful as you brother." "So you think I am successful brother?" Yes, I think you are successful." "What is your name my brother he said from behind the prison glass?" "Well my real name is Michael Jones but my nicknames are Mississippi or Sip."

"What is your birth name Twin?" "Well, I still have the same last name as you brother, my name is Mike Jones and they call me Chicago." "I found out years ago I was abducted from a hospital in Mississippi however the documents never said I had a twin brother." "I was at home one day getting ready for school and the police knocked on the door and arrested my mother." This was a terrible ordeal for me, now I didn't have my mother before this I was a straight a student preparing to go to college."

"I became angry and tried to repay everyone back, I did not realize that nobody did anything at all to me." My so-called mother was busted when I applied for a medicaid card but she couldn't provide the right social security number. "The feds were alerted when mother tried this and she was arrested at once." "I turned to a life of crime because I was so angry inside." I felt I had been robbed of my life, integrity and I felt I had nothing at all to lose. "Time is up." yelled the jailer. "Ok brother I will come back to see you next visit and I am sorry that you as well had to go through this terrible ordeal being switched at birth, I am sure it was an uncompromising position."

"Ok my brother, stay up I will see you on next visit."

Mississippi left New York prison facilities he went through the checkpoint clearances and headed home. Even though he left behind an identical twin brother, he could forgive him because his brother had no evil intentions to hurt him at all because his twin knew nothing about him at all.

This made is easy to forgive his brother. Meanwhile back in Queens Sip had to find a new job, well the only thing he knew now was construction.

The state cleared his name and he had no

felonies, he was exonerated. Some good news was coming his way there was a new law in New York that compensated you, if you were locked up or retained against your will in the state and he had been falsely accused of a crime he didn't commit. This new law was called the reparations act of 2000. Mississippi's car had been towed to the tow yard for the long stint he was in jail so he caught the bus down town to city hall to pick up his check and he was awarded 20,000.00 with installment payments of 6,000 a month he was scheduled to receive every month.

He saw the first check for 20,000.00 written out payable to Michael Jones. His next payment was set to hit his direct deposit every month. He was all set it appeared but he had some mental issues after discovering he had a long lost identical twin brother also he had nightmares at night from his stint in prison. Since Michael was free he didn't have to worry about a job so he attended a private outpatient mental illness hospital to get his mind right. One night before going to bed he noticed his phone ranged and the caller id read it was from his old friend New York. Usually he would answer his partner call on the first ring. He said to himself, "I ought to let the phone ring just like he let the phone ring for me when I was incarcerated."

The phone rang constantly but when it was about to go to voicemail Sip answered the phone and said "Hello how are you?" Said New York. "I am fine doing fine." Sippi in his heart loved his friend but he had a hard time forgiving him for not being by his side when he was arrested.

Mississippi had a hard time forgiving him because he really thought it was him who committed these horrible crimes, instead it was his unknown twin brother. The two old friends collaborated back and forth about old times in Webb M.S. also they shared some laughs and promised to see each other again.

Ch. 6   Urban City Lights

Life in New York is about bright lights and a city that never sleep. You can get what you want at 3 am in the morning. You could buy cannabis or go to your favorite restaurant early in the morning at 3 am also. It was a city that never slept.

It was fast urban living city. The business man wearing suits, he knows how to survive even the preacher they all know how to survive in the urban community. The turn and exchange for drug dealers, prostitutes, everyone knew how to make money and survive. The hustle is the same way no matter where you go or what city you live in. There was a saying in

New York and one of them was, "Fair exchange is no robbery." The other saying was, "Get it how you Live." Whether you went to church every Sunday or whether you shot dice on Friday night the hustle was understood and everything exchanged hands equally or you could not survive in this urban New York Community.

There were tall lights and tall buildings, which lights up and looks pretty at night. You could also go to the baseball stadium and watch a baseball game. On New Year's Eve on times square you could watch the ball drop.

There were many things to do in New York, you could watch the NBA play basketball. It is the city of dreams and how you play your hand determines how you will survive. New York had pimps with leather suits and feather in their hats. There is a lot of activity that occurs in New York but it is necessary that you mind your own business and stay in your own lane. In the city never go by your real government name. You should always go by a nick name, this is why New York went by the name of N.Y. on the street and Mississippi went by his code name Sip or Sippi.

If somebody is ever looking for you and they come to your ghetto, or urban community and ask your real name, no one can tell them any information about where you are.

This is why you always go by nickname and never tell the people in the community or project your real government name. Someone could be looking for you to kill you. Always choose an alias name to go by like El, Snake, Kool, slick etc. If someone comes to your community and ask for William Johnson, shouldn't no one even know him especially when he has told everyone his nickname is snake.

Your identity is very important in living in Urban Community. Many people go to a large state for exile because they are running from something in their own state. They may not be running form the government in their state or country but a large city like New York will hide them form their predator's.

In order to remain incognito this is why most people go by a nickname instead of the real government name. Another way to survive in New York is to close your mouth because if you open your mouth about everything you see, someone will close your mouth for you. I live by the rule that an old man once told me and that was, "See it and don't see it." Act like you don't see it when the pimp slaps the old man to the ground. You can open your mouth if you want to but you have to make a choice whether to help the old man or get the same punishment he gets. Well nothing has changed about the big apple.

The people at wall street invest money, the wealthy gets paid, the middle and poor class gets paid. City buses runs twenty-four hours a day.

The shelter was a big warehouse capable of holding over 3,000 people. You could really live and survive in N.Y. City if your mind and hustle was right. It was all about the hustle, the fast hustle. The early bird gets the worm and if you get up too late you will miss out. Things happened fast in this Urban city so you better keep your eyes focused and you better not slip is an old phrase commonly used in this city. Everything happened in this city from counterfeit money to crooked dice but it is not up to you to choose who is wrong. Keep minding your business and act like you didn't see the robbery or the murder because next you are the one to die.

New York was what you made it and it was certainly no place for a nosey person. There was a saying someone might send a kite on you.

This is not an actual kite that you fly in the sky. A kite is called a letter written to someone explaining to another person that you have wronged them. A kite could inform a person about your location and get you killed. This is what you call an invisible hit since the letter to harm you was written however you didn't know anything about it. One thing New York people will do if they feel you have crossed the line or insulted them. They will call their people, which is putting a hit out on you.

If you open your mouth in this city whether urban, suburbs, flats, streets, industrial courts you are only getting a hit put out on yourself. If you live by the golden rule which is minding your business in New York, you will live longer.

Meanwhile Sip received a letter while living in Queens, stating his daughter Amanda Was playing Ball for the WNBA in New York, this made him a proud father. New York two kids, Lysdney and C.J. received bachelor's degrees and was professors teaching at the college in New York. Things may happen in your life whether in the city, rural urban, county or any place. You cannot call the shots in your life no matter what city or county you live in. You may plan something in your life but it may not happen by design.

These parents New York and Sip was struggling to educate their children and their kids was kicked out of school and had to relocate to another city down south called Webb M.S. Now their children have made it to the WNBA and also chosen a career as professional teachers. Somethings the bottom rises to the top but you cannot call this. Life does not happen by design. What I am saying is, there were bruises along the way things didn't start out perfectly fine well neither will life. No one is perfect in life and no one is worst in life. There is good and bad in everyone. Even in the bad person you will find some good qualities. Life is like a percentage and ratio, life is like taking a chance. It is just like the roll of the dice you could hit lucky seven on first try or you could crap. Life is the chance you take, breathe is giving to you by God but life is a chance.

The hustle is a chance. Whether you hang with the best of the men or you hang with someone who everyone hates life is the same, the results are the same.

There are no short cuts to life the only things a short cut will lead to is the penitentiary or the grave.

No one is exempt from problems no matter where they live, the state or location cannot cause a problem. Life is a trail and trial occurs.

It makes no difference if you were living in New York or Mississippi. Another factor that could affect the trial you are going through is how you act during your trial. If you fight your trial, you could make it worst. If you can live in the city you can make it in the south. New York was a lovely place to live. Buffalo New York is very pretty when it snows.

New York has everything from the professional well-dressed man to the man sleeping on the ground and like any other city, there is this one guy or girl standing in front of the store begging for change. A county or city do not determine whether you survive or not, what determines if you survive or not in any place is yourself. Everything was going great in life on the surface so it seems. Everything in life appeared to be going just fine with Sip and New York but just because things are going fine doesn't mean it will stay that way. Life is precarious and unpredictable. Sometimes we make it to the finish line just to start the race all over again.

The questions were now, is this relationship with the two close friends irreparable? Keep in mind Mississippi is thinking like a criminal now. If you keep a man locked up long enough he will act like a criminal. On the other hand, the anger and resentment is hidden from his buddy New York and he doesn't even have a clue his partner hasn't forgiving him. On the other hand, New York was still involved in helping little children in the community.

He has been involved because he has a small ministry. One of N.Y. project was to help this little African girl who had leukemia and needed a lung transplant. The only way her family could get the money was to ask for help. New York being a community activist since a little boy started a fund account online and raise 300, 000 dollars. Little did New York know evil was brewing in his friend's head. The little girl's family was glad their sickly daughter could now finally receive a lung transplant and be saved.

New York consulted with the hospital and told them he had the money for the transplant and was ready to pay for the little's girl kidney replacement. N.Y. went to get the money it was too much money to carry around so he had the fund company too write him a check in the amount for three hundred thousand dollars. He was successful, he headed to the hospital to provide the check for the little girl kidney transplant, she was about 6 years old. Everything was going fine until he was side swiped by a vehicle and ran off the road.

It was a set up by his old partner Mississippi who had listened to the demons in his head long enough. The jail ways had taken over Sip and he wanted revenge on his old partner for betraying him. The police saw the accident and they arrested Sip and New York because they couldn't see who started the incident.

Sip hired someone to run over New York in a car to make it look like an accident because he betrayed him and left him in the jail to rot. Now this was a problem because New York has been checked into jail and he has the check for 300,000 dollars in his pockets to pay for the little African America girl kidney transplant.

Everything was all scheduled, the girl was prepped for surgery and ready for the kidney transplant which arrived by airplane for surgery. Sip was incarcerated again for causing the accident with New York out of revenge. Jealously is dangerous and so is trying to seek revenge.

Everything is on the line and time is running out

especially for the little six years old African American girl awaiting a lung transplant. Every time the physician called New York phone to pay for the transplant his phone went to voicemail, he was locked up. Time was running out being locked in jail but New York had to think fast. All of a sudden while N.Y. was sitting in jail with his face in his hands, his old buddy the captain was still at the jail precinct.

New York told his captain friend that he has a small ministry and he has a girl who is awaiting surgery in 45 minutes and he needed to get the check to the hospital to pay for the transplant. He explained if he is not there on time the kidney could be return to England and be disposed of and the little girl certainly would die. His friend the captain obtained the check and handed it to N.Y. He told the prisoner, "I will pop the back lock for you and turn off the cameras."

"No one is here but me, I will just tell the staff on first shift we had a problem with the cameras." His Captain friend also explained to him, "If he is not back in custody by eight am he will have to put an escape charge out on him." "I will be back before then." He replied. The door to the back of the jail was popped and soon as it was opened New York saw nothing but darkness and time was running out very fast.

There was no time to call a cab to make it to the hospital he had to make it on feet. He was released in his street clothes when a lady asked him did he need a ride. He said breathing very hard, "Take me to Clyde Ville Hospital."

"The old lady said, "My what is the urgency, what is wrong with you?" He explained, "I have to make it to the hospital in time to provide this check so a little girl could have a kidney transplant." The little 80-year- old lady said, "Well I am driving the best that I can" The physician said, "Well the lung is on ice and is in perfectly good shape, but I cannot do the transplant unless someone is here to pay for it. The little girl was lying on the stretcher needing the surgery very badly. Things were looking dim, the girl was actually dying and fading away fast.

There were tears in her mother eyes. When all of a sudden she saw a middle aged white guy running down the hall yelling, "I'm here, I made it with the 300,000 dollar check." The mother tears dried up and the fear of death was erased off the little girl's face.

New York handed the check to the physician and the little girl was taken back into surgery, the operation was a success. N.Y. made it back to the jail in time to be counted. The captain placed a dummy in the bed to be counted for him. The mother of the little girl went to thank New York but he was gone. In her mind she said he was an angel because only angels do good deeds and disappear. Ironically N.Y. made it back to the jail in time because his court hearing was beginning to start in tweeny-minutes.

His friend captain attended his court proceeding to make his presence seen. The inmate told the court, "I was run over by a friend who is mad at me because he thinks I betrayed him." "It was my friend who caused the accident." "I

was headed to the hospital to pay for a kidney

transplant when I was side swiped by three men in a

car and one of the men was Mississippi." "His real

name is Michael Jones." "I am telling you I am

innocent." The jury believed his story and made him a

free man however they had no evidence of the crime

so they had to set his friend Michael free as well. Both

of the men were released and set free. Michael caused

the accident and injuries to his friend but life is not

fair. Mississippi was not the same anymore since he

had been wrongfully incarcerated.

The torture didn't stop there were shots fired at

N.Y. home and you could hear the sounds of skids

marks from a car that speeded off real fast. Well New

York and taken enough, he sold his home his children were already professors at a New York college and could now take care of Themselves.

He was afraid of Sip now because he could see a change in him and he knew betrayal was dangerous. He informed his daughter Lyndsey and his son C.J. that his partner Mississippi had lost his mind and stay away from him and do not inform him any information on his whereabouts.

New York secretly sold his house and moved back to Webb M.S. He had to lay low from exile in a small town. Sometimes when you hiding from exile you can hide in a large city but this time N.Y. had to hide in a small town.

Well He arrived in Webb early Saturday Morning,

he was happy to see the town just where he left it. All the stores were still standing and the people were still standing in front of the washer having a good time as usual. He ran into his old friend Dollar Bob who didn't recognize him. N.Y. spoke to him and he said, "Hello city man, I did not recognize you without your friend with you." "Where is your friend called Chicago?"

"No actually his name was Mississippi." "Well he decided not to come with me this time, he is happy in New York City." The town embraced New York, they already knew him as being part of the ones who constructed most of the stores in the town.

The mayor of Webb Mr. Livingston recognized New York right away. He told N.Y., "Welcome back to the small town of Webb Sir, it is good to have you back." Mr. Livingston asked the northerner, "Do you need a job." "Well I could use a freelance job because I have bought a house in Goosepond."

New York took his time but he built more stores in Webb over a six-year period, there was a mall built in Webb and people from other surroundings counties came to shop. The people came from Charleston, Tutwiler Rome, Clarksdale, Cleveland Mississippi and etc. Everything was the same in Mississippi Dollar Bob was still dancing in the town and smiling. He had his drink in his hands but he wasn't bothering no one.

The town didn't know that there was beef between old friends and they certainly didn't know that N.Y. was hiding in the small town of Webb from exile and he feared for his life.

He returned to living in the Goosepond subdivision consisting of brick building once known as brick city. This time he was living on the 3rd street near the back. He was comfortable living in exile at least for now. New York received a phone call while sitting in his car up town, it was an area code form his hometown. The phone call was from the little girl he saved with the kidney transplant The little girl mother wanted to thank him for raising the money to give her daughter a transplant.

The little African American girl was named Princess and was now thirteen years old. She became a ballerina girl for the Olympic and won two Olympic gold medals. Joy came into his heart and he told her

Mother God bless you and always stay in touch with me.

Ch. 7   New York And Mississippi Returns To Webb

M.S.

It seems like Mississippi should have been comfortable living life in New York because his friend who he believed had betrayed him was not there. He was dealing with mental issues caused by living in the jail. He was hearing voices again. Prison life left him stir crazy now he was back out on the street.

Sip walked outside and fired his weapon in the air when no one was outside. The neighbors called the police and the police were summoned to his home. He, "told the police he was shooting at the man outside." The police asked him, "Where is the man?"

"He is standing over there." The police responded, "There is no man standing over there." "We have ran your name and you suffer from mental illness and been incarcerated before if we come back over here, we will have you face some severe jail time."

The doctor found a drug to help the patient who suffer from depression of any type, the doctors offered it to Mississippi, and it helped him greatly. Now he has started to gain his composure and mind back. Sip realized now that he had three felonies now.

He was a habitual criminal and was able to face some serious time if he was ever caught in trouble again. He remembered all the chaos that jail caused him so he figured it would be best for him to leave the state because he wanted to stay a free man especially with the new drug that was administered to him to help him with depression. Ironically, he was thinking just like his old friend New York whom he had fell on bad terms with.

He had a little money left but with him being a three times habitual offender the state had set a date in five months for his benefits to expire because he would then be a habitual offender. He was ok to get a job or anything at this point but in five months all benefits received from the state would expire.

The state of New York had a law that did not support habitual offenders. The very next day Sip went to the doctors to have his new medicine transferred to Sumner Mississippi pharmacy. This medicine made him practically brand new, he didn't hear any more voices or see things that was not there.

The next move was he informed his daughter Amanda who was in her third with the WNBA, he informed her of the new medicine he received that help him keep his composure.

Sip then informed Amanda that he had to move back down south to keep his insanity. He told her that he was tired of repeatedly going to jail and he wanted to live a better life maybe go to church and find God and she was perfectly fine with the idea and supported her father.

Everything was set in place even his bank account had been routed to Webb M.S. Michael arrived in Webb, he wanted to live in the country so he moved by the bridge in the outstretch of Webb on route to Charleston M.S. He figured living down a dirt road would be very quiet since he had been through a terrible ordeal mentally. No one really knew Sip had moved back to Webb and this is how he wanted it. One day he went to buy some food and The Mayor of Webb Mr. Livingston recognized him said, "How are you doing?" "I am glad you made it back to Webbs." Sippi shook his hands and moved away fast he had nothing against the mayor but he didn't want to make any friends in the town. He was hit with a bombshell when the mayor informed him that New York had moved back as well. "Oh yea," said Michael trying to play innocent.

He didn't want any trouble while living in exile. New York was also living in Webb in exile but he didn't know his old friend had moved back. Sometimes exile will slow a person down and cause him to live straight because no one wants to be discovered or recognized. Sip knew New York was back in town but New York didn't know Sip had moved back. It didn't matter the two old friends had to chalk it up and get on with their lives' separately now. Finally, one day the two met in Sumner M.S. at the pharmacy when Sip arrived there to pick up his medication he needed to rely on to help him function mentally.

Once the old friends' eyes made contact it was a shock for N.Y. but not for his partner Mississippi because Mr. Livingston the mayor had already informed him New York had moved back. It was a total shock to New York to see his old buddy because they were on bad terms, it didn't matter now. Sometimes life is a 360 turn around and things don't stay the same. People fall out but they have to outweigh the situation, which is more important getting into trouble or living a normal life. We have to make the best decisions in life sometimes we get a chance to fix things in our lives' and sometimes we don't.

Well meanwhile Sip went home to a life in the country to shut himself inside the house and mind his own business. He walked to the mailbox and received a letter that Acme railroad country wanted to build a casino across his land and tear down all the house in the country in about nine months.

The Webb native obtained a lawyer and asked him how can he stop Acme railroad Company from building a casino across his property and tear down all the house in the country. His lawyer told him that there was nothing he could do about it but leave because the property he was living on was private property owned by Mr. Johnson. The Acme Railroad Company was able to buy out the property from the property owner without paying him one cent. Sip was going through another trial and he was bracing himself not to panic through the trial.

He remembered in four months from now, he was scheduled to be a habitual criminal, then he wouldn't be able to get a job so he better act fast now before his criminal record set in. He was a free man as of now so he applied for work at the prison. He was accepted at the penitentiary as prison guard. He finally found something he liked, no one in the south knew he had been locked up before. No he didn't like guarding people because he was locked up himself before. He finally found something he was good act. One day in training to become a correctional officer the final test was to pass a shooting course. Everyone lined up to shoot targets with a mini 14 riffle. The beginning cadets were taken up on a two story building and were told to shoot the targets way across the field about 40 yards away.

Some of the cadets could not see on the top of the building however once Sip learned the routine he hit all 20 out of 20 shots. Once he heard the gun bust the first time this was music to his ears and he loved it. Some cadets failed the shooting course because they were wearing glasses and could not see.

The instructor proceeded to the next phase at the shooting range which was on the ground. The target was placed up and the cadets were instructed to shoot the target placed out across the field at long range. It was also a success Michael hit all ten shots. Sip had a perfect shooting record at this point. The next phase of shooting at the range was a moving target however, the instructor did not tell the cadets that it was a moving target. Mississippi had the mini 14 weapon placed firmly under his arms and leaned forward to shoot the target, he hit the moving target three times and missed it two times only because he wasn't told it was a moving target.

He was shooting well than the sergeant so the

instructor asked him to train the other students and they passed their test which was required at the range and they became officers. Michael had a job now at least until the state of New York issued he was a habitual offender. The state of Mississippi laws were you could not hold any government job as a habitual offender. It worked about four months as he predicted before the habitual offender news would hit the state of M.S. The Webb resident received a letter in the mailbox stating that the property he was living on was scheduled to be renovated by bulldozers in one week to prepare the land for a casino to be built, by then Sip had been through enough.

Now he was jobless again and about to have no place to stay again. In one week the bulldozers lined up on the property to tear down the buildings for construction when they noticed one tenant was not evacuated from the building. The bulldozer approached forward to tear down the building. The tenant refused to leave as his mind went back to the training session he had with the mini 14 weapon back at the penitentiary. Mississippi did not surrender to the Acme Rail Road Company who did not know they would face fierce resistance from a trained sharp shooter.

Sippi was in a military stance, he had death on his mind. He remembered down south while living in Greenville M.S. that a sharecropper took his grandmother money from sharecropping and didn't give her one dime. He said, "You will not take everything I got I don't have no place to go." The southerner had flashbacks from the penitentiary and fired fourteen shots with his mini fourteen rifle and disabled the bulldozer but no one was injured or hurt. Once the word was out that disgruntle tenant was a professional sharp shooter from the prison, the national guard was called in to disable him. He said repeatedly, "If anyone tries to take my property it will be over my dead body, I have exhausted all options." The scene unfolded by the bridge in Webb Mississippi. Sip had disabled the bulldozer, the railroad sent for back up.

The National Guard swarmed the place by helicopter and by land but they could not see because the helicopter was blowing the dirt which made a thick cloud of dust and no one could see. The captain said, "Take the chopper out of the sky, it is blowing up too much dust on this dirt road." However, the now southerner had a military stance and hate was in his eyes. This incident unfolded worldwide on the evening news and his old friend New York saw it all unfold." N.Y. jumped into his car and made it to the scene, which was taped off. The National Guard told to him to stay back or he would be detained.

He then rushed passed the barricades to help Sip. When Michael saw him, I guess he saw the love in his partner's reaction because no one would defy the National Guard's orders and come to his rescue. Immediately he told N.Y. to stop running before he steps on one of the land mine he set for the intruders.

New York stopped in his tracks once he heard this and told his longtime partner Mississippi, "No one can take everything you got because they can't take me from you." "We are all we got partner until death do us part." Sip dropped the mini 14 weapon and hugged New York until they both began crying. New York was right, they were all they had. Mr. Livingston, the mayor of Webb then entered the scene and yelled to the National Guard, "Everything is fine here and everyone needs to go home now." The good deeds the guys did in the town came to their rescue.

These guys had built stores in the town and restored the economy. The mayor was able to put in a good word for Sip and New York to stop what they were facing which was death and destruction. See sometimes in life you win and sometimes in life you lose. We fall out with people but sometimes the same people we fall out with are the same people who will help us succeed, see sometimes life is precarious it is not predictable.

You may live your whole life flawless until you make one mistake only to see everyone leave you or betray you, see sometimes life makes no excuses for you and life does not care who you are and like New York said, "Jealously is dangerous but love is powerful." You may live your life but you will never live your life like New York and Sip did. Sometimes in life, somebody will have to say a good word for you like the mayor said for New York and Sip. I would rather you say a good word for me now while I am living, rather than you say a good word for me at my funeral. Jealously is dangerous but betrayal is even worst. How many people will leave me for dead or how many people will stick up for me? I may never know, I just might end up living my whole life like New York and Sip.